LIBRARIAN REVIEWER
Laurie K. Holland
Media Specialist (National Board Certified), Edina, MN
MA in Elementary Education, Minnesota State University, Mankato, MN

READING CONSULTANT
Elizabeth Stedem
Educator/Consultant, Colorado Springs, CO
MA in Elementary Education, University of Denver, CO

Graphic Sparks are published by Stone Arch Books,
151 Good Counsel Drive, P.O. Box 669,
Mankato, Minnesota 56002.
www.stonearchbooks.com

Library of Congress Cataloging-in-Publication Data
Nickel, Scott.
    The Boy Who Burped Too Much / by Scott Nickel; illustrated by Steve Harpster.
    p. cm. — (Graphic Sparks)
    ISBN-13: 978-1-59889-037-2 (hardcover)
    ISBN-10: 1-59889-037-9 (hardcover)
    ISBN-13: 978-1-59889-168-3 (paperback)
    ISBN-10: 1-59889-168-5 (paperback)
    1. Graphic novels. I. Harpster, Steve. II. Title. III. Series.
PN6727.N544B69 2006
741.5—dc22   2005026693

Summary: Bobby Aaron was a cool kid, but not a normal kid. His burps were
uncontrollable. He belched at the movies, erupted in the library, and even blasted away in
the principal's office. Bobby needs to keep his cool and squelch his belches in order to win
the spelling bee. But then he runs into Courtney, another word for "trouble." Gulp!

Art Director: Heather Kindseth
Production Manager: Sharon Reid
Production/Design: James Liebman, Mie Tsuchida
Production Assistance: Bob Horvath, Eric Murray

1 2 3 4 5 6 11 10 09 08 07 06

THE BOY WHO BURPED TOO MUCH

BY SCOTT NICKEL

ILLUSTRATED BY STEVE HARPSTER

STONE ARCH BOOKS
Minneapolis   San Diego

CAST OF CHARACTERS

Joseph

Grandpa

Courtney Williams

Bobby Aaron was a normal kid.

17

ABOUT THE AUTHOR

Scott Nickel has written children's books, short fiction for *Boys' Life Magazine*, humorous greeting cards, and lots of really funny knock-knock jokes. Scott is also the author of many Garfield books.

Currently, Scott lives in Indiana with his wife, two sons, four cats, a parakeet, and several sea monkeys.

ABOUT THE ILLUSTRATOR

Steve Harpster has loved drawing funny cartoons, mean monsters, and goofy gadgets since he was able to pick up a pencil. In first grade, he was able to avoid his writing assignments by working on the pictures for stories instead.

Steve landed a job drawing funny pictures for books, and that's really what he's best at. Steve lives in Columbus, Ohio, with his wonderful wife, Karen, and their sheepdog, Doodle.

GLOSSARY

aqua (AH-kwa) water or the color greenish-blue; not to be confused with the Spanish word agua, which also means "water"

catastrophe (kuh-TASS-truh-fee) a disaster or a terrible event, such as losing your lucky rubber frog during a spelling bee or burping a tuna-fish sandwich out your nose

llama (LAH-muh) a large, camel-like mammal that lives in South America

mackerel (MAK-ur-uhl) a shiny blue fish that lives in the ocean; eating too much mackerel can make you burp. Fish burps! Now that's a real catastrophe.

spelling bee (SPEL-ing BEE) a contest where people have to spell words correctly, such as the word "correctly"

Read it!
Read it!

BURP BLURBS

Burps are caused by something you can't even see – air. The average person swallows a cup of air a day. Some people swallow as much as 10 cups a day!

Foods release gas in your stomach. Gas can make you burp, too. Foods that contain the most gas are milk, apples, nuts, onions, sauerkraut, and soda pop.

When you are nervous, you swallow more air than normal. Then you burp!

When the air or gas in your stomach escapes through your mouth, you start burping. Doctors call it by a bigger name. They say you are ERUCTATING (uh-RUK-tay-ting).

The world's loudest burp was recorded at more than 118 decibels (DESS-uh-buhls). That's louder than the buzz of a chain saw!.

The best way to prevent burping is to stop swallowing so much air. Here are some real-life cures for preventing or getting rid of burps.

1.) Don't drink fizzy drinks, like soda pop.

2.) Don't use a straw when you drink.

3.) Don't gulp down liquids. Sip them slowly.

4.) Chew with your mouth closed.

DISCUSSION QUESTIONS

1.) Bobby burps everywhere. Do you think he really can't help it, or is he making excuses?

2.) Bobby's grandpa gives him his lucky Frog to help him stop burping. Do you think the Frog was really lucky, or was Grandpa only pretending?

3.) Courtney was upset when she stepped on Bobby's Frog on the stage. Did that make her lose the spelling bee? Who do you think is the better speller?

WRITING PROMPTS

1.) Bobby's burps make a lot of noise! Write a story describing a strange or funny sound that you can make with your mouth, and the trouble it gets you into.

2.) Grandpa's lucky Frog helped him win a year's supply of macaroni and cheese. Write a story that tells how you win a contest and what the prize is.

3.) Bobby's Friend tries to help him stop burping. What if you couldn't stop burping, either? Write down what your Friends would do to try and cure you. Do any of the cures work?

INTERNET

Do you want to know more about subjects related to this book? Or are you interested in learning about other topics? Then check out FactHound, a fun, easy way to find Internet sites.

Our investigative staff has already sniffed out great sites for you!

Here's how to use FactHound:

1.) Visit www.facthound.com

2.) Select your grade level.

3.) To learn more about subjects related to this book, type in the book's ISBN number: **1598890379**. If you're looking for information on another subject, simply type in a keyword.

4.) Click the **Fetch It** button.

FactHound will fetch the best Internet sites for you.

www.**FactHound**.com
SM